Wonders

WINNER OF THE
WALT WHITMAN AWARD FOR 1978

Sponsored by the Academy of American Poets,
the Walt Whitman Award is given annually to the
winner of an open competition among American poets who
have not yet published their first book of poetry.
The 1978 award was supported by an anonymous donor.
Judge for 1978: Louis Simpson.

Wonders

Karen Snow

THE VIKING PRESS

NEW YORK

Library of Congress Cataloging in Publication Data
Snow, Karen.   Wonders.   I. Title.
PS3569.N62W6   811'.5'4   79-20439
ISBN 0-670-77917-2

Printed in the United States of America
Set in CRT Baskerville

The following poems originally appeared in
The Beloit Poetry Journal :
"Apples," "Afterglow," "Low,"
"Grit," "Snow" (as "Snow Falls on Flowers"),
"Wonders" (as "Messages"),
"Tit for Tat," "Whitey," "Clover," and "Whelping."

"Kindergarten" originally appeared in the *Michigan Quarterly Review.*

"Thirteen" originally appeared in *Parade* and is reprinted here with
their permission. Copyright © Parade Publications, 1962.

In memory of Louis Untermeyer

Contents

Wonders

Clover

"She's her daddy's girl!" my aunt called
from the back seat of the clackety Model-T.
I was in front, on my dad's lap, next to
Uncle Lester, who was driving.
"She sure is her daddy's girl." Lester laughed.
I was four, sitting snug, jiggling, holding
my dad's thumb.

That was the day IT *started.*

We stopped at a ramshackle one-room schoolhouse.
The door was open. We all got out and waded through
the tall grass—even my mother and my big sister Dora,
who were scared of snakes and crickets. Inside we saw
the rusty stove and some coat hooks and a shelf with a
tin can on top. Dad took it down—a big can with a lid
and a wire handle. He grinned. "Here's my dinner bucket."

"It is *not*," my mother said. "Anyway, it's a *lunch pail*."

My dad sighed. "Well, Lester, we can't go back to
those days." And he put the can back on the shelf.

"Don't start *that* stuff!" My mother huffed.

She was always mad at him. I never knew why.

Dad turned and went out the door. I thought he
was walking away from her, as I did sometimes,
to cry, and I hurried after him.
He stood, back to me, hands clasped behind,
looking out across a field of clover,
and I noticed his hair was getting gray.
A warm wind blew over the clover,
and I knew he was thinking about dying.

Then we all piled into the Model-T,
I on my dad's lap again, and Mamma and Dora
and my aunt and Cousin Maybelle in back,
and we went jiggling down the dusty road.
I could feel my dad's sad gaze wandering over
the fields of corn, the fields of wheat, the oats,
over the cows grazing, and the sheep, and the trees,
and over the blue sky and the peach-colored clouds,
and when we passed a field of clover and that sweetness
came over us, my heart hurt. *That was YOUR dinner
bucket*, I wanted to say, but I just rubbed the furry
back of his hand on my cheek.

A *smoothness* was gone.
There was a stick in my throat.
And I knew it was the clover-thing.
Sometimes I'd walk over to my dad and
take hold of his hand.

> "Hangin on yer dad all the time," my
> mother scolded. "What's the matter
> with ya, anyway?"

I was ashamed. I ought to be able to fix it,
like when the elastic in your pants breaks,
you can grab it quick and poke open the hem and
find the end and fasten it with a safety pin
and the pants will stay up good as ever.

> The next summer, when Uncle Lester came for us
> in the car, I felt sick. But I had to go along.
> We didn't go to the schoolhouse, but the fields
> and trees looked the same. And the stick moved
> in my throat. Everywhere—cornfields, wheat fields,
> pastures, trees, sky, clouds—where my dad's gaze
> had sown sadness last year, Sorrow had sprung up.
> Mostly in the fields of clover.

Maybe it's kinneygarden I'm worried about,
I told myself. *A mean teacher maybe and
mean boys and Daddy not there to say,*
"Leave her be."

But kindergarten wasn't bad. The teacher
was kind, and the boys weren't so mean.
Just dumb.

The next summer, the clover-thing was worse.
We didn't even see Lester, and nobody took us
out for a drive, but something—like termites—
was scraping at my throat.

Maybe it's first grade I'm worried about—

But first grade wasn't that bad.
I got *was* and *saw* mixed up and numbers
made me nervous, but most of the kids were
a lot dumber than me, and the teacher gave
me A's.

The next summer was worse.
My dad looked sadder and grayer.
Sometimes when he was shaving at the
kitchen sink or reading the newspaper
or staking tomatoes, I'd just go stand
next to him.

"That man's got no more use fer you n
he has fer me. Can't ya *see* that?"
my mother whispered. "He's all *Dora*.
The sun rises n the sun sets in *Dora*."

I thought maybe I could get Dora on my side
against the clover-thing. So one day when I

found her alone, I sneaked it on her: "I feel
so sorry for Daddy," I began.

"Me too."

"He's so *old*."

"And Mamma treats him rotten."
And she dashed off to play Rin-Tin-Tin
with her pals.

It felt like termites, even in my stomach,
but maybe that was the Devil working.
So I prayed.

In second grade kids started calling me
"Skinny." The school nurse said, "Why!
You haven't gained one ounce!" I thought
maybe it was my Cross-to-Bear. But then
I didn't think God would lay that on you
before high school.... It was really
more like termites— No, like ants, building sandy bumps.

Please, God, I prayed, *it's been three
years, going on four. Fix this clover-
thing.*

When my dad carried the Christmas tree into
the living room, and Dora started to pull on
it, my mother whispered to me,

"Those two don't want you n me interferin.
Can't ya tell?" She went to the kitchen
to cry, as she always did on holidays, for
her father, who was dead. I could never

4

make myself care about her crying. It was
like the dust on the floor.

I went right in and sat on the couch.
(*God wants me to see this sunrise-sunset.*)
Dad and Dora argued about which branches
to the front and which to the wall. They
strung up the lights without a word, until
Dora said, "All blue ones this year."

Dad said—with a very slight grin and with
a sigh, too—"You're the boss." Then he sat
in his chair and opened his Bible.
Dora screwed in the blue bulbs and hung the
baubles and then she asked me to help with the
tinsel.   That was all.
No, not all: The tree smelled of clover.
Which didn't surprise me.

I grew too tall to sit on my dad's lap for
those few summer drives, and I grew too stiff
to take hold of his hand or even to look at him
much. The clover-thing stayed the same.
I'd think, *Oh, well, maybe after fourth grade
. . . or maybe after fifth . . . or maybe if
I gain some weight—*
I drank a lot of Ovaltine,

which may have helped. I got all A's
and even some A pluses.

O.K., Smarty, I said to myself. *Get to work
on this clover-conundrum. Look: That sweet
smell of clover coming toward you is a BALL,
and before you can catch it, this BAT (Daddy will
die) pops up and whacks it away.
Grab that bat.*

Which was dumb.
It was the worst summer yet.
My dad got grayer, and he started
to cough. His chair that had smelled
of creosote wafted clover.

Dear God, DO something—

Those ants were pushing my shoulder blades
out and making me shaky. A neighbor said
to my mother, "Your younger daughter is
starting to resemble you."

Dear God, don't let my life go bad,
like my mother's—

The prayer dropped through a sand trap.
Those ants had packed me a brimful of bumps.
They climbed right out on my face and
nailed up their little NO VACANCY smile.

Grit

"Think of someone worse off n yerself,"
snaps my mother.

 I droop on the couch.

"An wipe that look off yer face!"

 I try to go blank.

Brandishing a mop,
she thrusts her face into the doorway.
The eyes—one brown, one gray—stare at me.
"If there's one thing I can't stand,
it's a *baby*."
And the nose is humped.
She looks like the puppet Punch.
She retreats to the kitchen.
Wham! goes the pail.
Splat! goes the mop.

 The text for today:
 Tenderness is taboo.

Fumes of ammonia leap toward me like
a noose.
Bang. Whomp. Swat.

Dark Dora brushes by the couch.
Out of the side of her mouth
she says, "Think of snowflakes."
Then she goes out the door, to school.

The Punch-face pokes around the doorway again.
"I wish you had jest haff o that girl's *grit*.

She was twice as sick as you, for three days;
threw up from the soles o her feet, everthing
but her toenails. Cleaned up every mess by
herself. Her face's yellow as butter. Didn't
ya notice? But she goes ta school, anyway."

I wilt.

"Yer thinkin of *yourself!*
Think of someone *else!*"
She pops back into the kitchen.
More ammonia.

Another mother would be
laying a soft palm on my forehead,
offering pale tea or orange juice.
I should be glad she doesn't try
to soothe me. Her hands are like
alligators. ("*When I was sixteen,
I asked for some lemon hand cream
for Christmas, n my brothers pissed
in a bottle n give it ta me. Ha,
I laughed. I can take a joke.*")

Re-enter Alligator:
"Why, where would *I* be if *I* thought
about myself: In the 'sylum, that's where.
Or in the grave. What would *you* do if *you*
had my laxeration floppin b'tween yer legs
all the time, *huh*? That's what I've had ta
put up with ever since givin birth ta Dora."

I've heard this a hundred times.
I picture a cubed steak, of moderate size,
flapping from her crotch.
Her big bloomers accommodate it.

8

Exit Alligator, to the kitchen.
Sounds of huffing and puffing and of the mop
bludgeoning the cellar steps.

Somewhere nuns are saying their beads.

She calls out, "Dr. Tenbrink said,
'I don't know how you stand it, Mrs. Von Musson.
You could sue the doctor that left you in
that shape!' "

A chair topples.
"But I'm too bashful to show myself
in a courtroom. An I don't think about it.
I think about Minnie Huyser. She's nearly
seventy. Her organs are hangin almost
to her *knees!* Think of *that!*
Someday they'll pull the bladder right outa her!"
Splat.

I picture a wad of chicken parts
on a purplish thong, like a pendulum,
tolling away Minnie Huyser's days.

Another noose of ammonia.
The toilet gulps down the pail of mop water.

("Yer no good! What'll I do with ya?
Huh? Shall I throw ya away? Huh?
Aw, wipe that look off yer face!
It's just a game!" —Memories of
playful baby-days.)

Now the odor of Fels Naphtha soap.
My head throbs. My eyes sting. My throat
feels "laxerated." The washing machine,

in the cellar below me, growls with its
hugged prey. The wringer squeals.

Re-enter Punch.
She thrusts a glass of water at me.
"I spoil ya. Dora got her own, always."
She points to her temple. "See that?"

    I see nothing.

"Bumped it on the corner o the cellar door.
Isn't it red?"

    I nod.

"Soon it will be a lump—purple, green, blue.
I'll forget about it. Ha!"

    That *look* has come over her face.
    I brace myself: Here it comes:

"I hope ya don't turn out like yer Aunt Marie
—layin there cryin in that 'sylum. Hell,
a nurse oughta slip her a dose o somethin ta
give her a *real* bellyache n make her clean up
after herself. Give her sumpin *real* ta cry
about, huh?!"

    Snowflakes on you, Aunt Marie.

"Think of Aunt Ida. Her with a tumor like a
grapefruit in her side n others like a bunch
o grapes in her tit. She goes right on workin.
Yer cousin Freddie: hemorrhages from his nose
like cranberry sauce. He goes on drivin that
Hostess truck."

Her speciality, in technicolor, like a
slide show: Uncle Dan: skin disease like
raw hamburger all over his neck . . . Aunt
Elsie: goiter like a hen's egg . . . Aunt
Agnes: wad of fur the size of a cantaloupe
in her appendix ("For years, her pa *told* her
n *told* her not to keep kissin that cat!").

"Think of Uncle Casey's sinus trouble:
Why! ta look in that man's hankerchiefs,
you'd think he'd blowed out his *brains!*"

    snow   snow
    Sikes told her once of a carnival where
    he saw, among other heroics, a man pushing
    his nuts in a wheelbarrow: elephantiasis.
    Snowflakes and white roses and lilies of
    the valley, cover that wheelbarrow—

"An don't forget Uncle Klaus: The doctor in
the prison hospital told him drinkin's a *disease.*"
She taps her temple.   "Is it swelling?"

    I nod.

She lunges at the curtains, shakes them:
testing for dust.   Knocks a picture askew
on the wall.   It's Jesus in the Garden of
Gethsemane praying to God to cancel Good Friday.
She's getting hopped up now. This sublimation stuff
exhilarates her. "An the doctor said, 'Why, Mrs.
Von Musson, if you don't have that laxeration operated
on, you'll not last another five years.' Poo. Here
I am, cleanin the house. You know *why?* Because I
think of *others.*"
She snatches the Hoover.

They whizz around the room together
like a dance team.
"Sadie Morton!" she yells.
"Think of poor Sadie Morton!"

> Sadie Morton: Dead of consumption
> last year. *Snowflakes. A blanket
> of snow on your grave, Poor Sadie Morton.*

She's glowering at me.

> Has that babyish look seeped back into
> my face?

"I don't know what'll become o you, girl.
Just like yer father.   Just like his sister Marie.
Three sissies!"

> I turn my face from her,
> waiting for five-thirty,
> when my father's mournful glance
> will confirm my misery.

She slams the Hoover into the closet.
Her glance reevaluates my face.

> *C minus?*

She points a pistol-finger at her calf.
"What'dya do if *you* had legs like this?"

> I make myself look at that bunch
> of marbles in her stocking.

Jabbing that gun-finger: "What'd *you* do, *huh?*"

> *Shoot it?*

"Speak up. What would *you* do if *you* had
these veins?"

> *Wear slacks?*
> I shake my head, woefully.

A smile twitches at her lips.

> *I'm up to C plus?*

"I don't give them a thought.
I think of others. Right now, ya know
who I'm thinkin of?"

> I shake my head, humbly.

"Hank Plow. Did I ever tell ya bout
Hank Plow?"

> I nod, but too faintly.

"Hank Plow had his arm tore off in the cutter
at the paper mill. Gangrene set in—"

> *A blizzard of snow on your green stump,*
> *Hank Plow.*

"Then Hank's brother, Ernie, he had this
terrible accident—"

> I lie there, imprinted, her *tabula rasa.*

Those colored slides, which have rendered
me catatonic, have filled her with a helium.
Billowing with borrowed sufferings,
she seizes the stepladder. "I've a good mind
ta wash the ceiling!" she sings.

She mounts the rungs: *Minnie   Sadie   Casey.*
Halfway up, her red Aryan hands take a swipe
at the beige lampshade: *Marie   Dad   me.*
"My lump's turnin green now, isn't it? Ha!"

She soars to the ceiling
and scrubs the stains from her heaven.

Thirteen

Tall
like a god
and bronze-colored like a god, too,
he strolls in and announces in cello tones,
"This is American history
for grade eight, section A,
and I am Mr. Sinclair."

This utterance,
captured in blue ink in her notebook,
spirals into spires
she scarcely recognizes as her own.

He calls the roll:
"Richard Bachman . . . Johanna Nyboer
. . . Harold Toolstra . . ."
It's like finding under old leaves
the pearls of fungus.
". . . Wilhelmina Von Musson:
That's a big name for a small girl.
May I call you 'Willo'?"
In a flash—
like Saul on the road to Damascus—
she is reborn.

*

With the Industrial Revolution
crammed, like a locomotive,
into her trinket-shop mind;
with no breakfast for ballast,
she flutters
past the paper mill,
"Frederick! Frederick!"
down the railroad track,

"Frederick! Frederick!"
and her feet turn the ties
into piano keys.

*

Before class,
the girls jingle their bracelets.

"Yikes! He's a *Brain*."

"But conceited."

The girls screw their hair into curls.

"Jeez, I hate him."

"Me too."

That Bruce keeps shoving his arm
close to her to display
what he has printed on his grimy wrist:
N.R.A. WE DO OUR PART.

Willo sits holy as a lily,
letting the prepared statement
(*"I have a lot of respect for him"*)
bloom and blur . . . blur and bloom
behind the haze of her silence.

*

The joy has turned to torment:
Each morning's recitation is a stillbirth
of the evening's toil.
Added to the numb tongue,
the porcelain fingers;
to the porcelain fingers,
the arrow-tip breasts

breaking like pleurisy from baby-ribs;
to the arrow-tip breasts,
the pink shame speckling the forehead
beneath the skirt of bangs
. . . until her misery for him
is as obvious as the brittle posture
under the Midas-touch.

    *

Virginia—
big and bulbous,
with bold black armpits
like suction cups of yearning,
standing in her slip and sneakers—
whispers, "Guess what? Mr. Sinclair
was drinking at that double fountain
with me, and he got so close
I nearly had to slap his face."
Virginia—
pendulous and pouting,
shrugging electrically out of her slip
and standing in the satin puddle
with all the virtuosity
of her fourteen years.

    *

Next year,
or the next,
with violets in her hair
and with the sweet agony of Strauss
wringing the air,
she will torrent down the stairs,
spill suddenly into his arms,
and he will sink her sinew-deep
into his flesh, moaning,
"Willo! Willo!"

*

June tenth:
the beginning of the three-month drought,
when she will be parched
except for the one page
in this blue satin autograph book,
which Virginia has promised
to pass him at the end of the hour
with her prose-steady hand.

Tit for Tat

Nature made a mistake—or so it seemed—
when It drove a force through flesh
like a torpedo through mild waters.

There was Willo, dainty blonde,
with lullaby-voice and rock-a-bye walk;

and there was Margaret, rawboned redhead,
with rusty voice and what-the-hell stride.

These two met in high school.
Vehement gaze shot into cupped gaze,
and brimmed. Wool hand grazed silk hand;
fingers sizzled, caught, clung.
Sudden summer scorched their skins;
nipples budded through blouses.
In the darkened locker room, kisses burrowed;
tongues clove like snakes copulating.

The gym teacher blew her nose.
Then she blew her whistle.

A music mightier than a whistle
kept swiveling every cell of their flesh
into a rhapsody of opposites.
Yin invited yang;
yang explored yin.
Dazzled by their magic, they took
secret names: *Wella* and *Wand*.

All these implosions made them luminous.
They glided about like a pair of lamps
propelled by a gyroscope.

Snow

    snow   snow
I've never seen so much snow:
forest and field and farm souffléed in snow;
Snyder's Funeral Home like a huge wedding cake;
pink roses, blue larkspur wearing white bonnets;
all of us white-veiled by the blizzard
that Valentine's Day you married Death.

      Maybelle.   Wild cousin.   Ripe sixteen.
      Bride.   I caught your bouquet.

What I mean is: I had already memorized you:
That summer you were fourteen and I was twelve,
you pendulumed back and forth in that swing,
back and forth before me, like a hypnotist:
your lacquered lashes swooping up and down,
up and down over those chicory-blue eyes, like
bird wings   your amber mane galloping
that cologne swarming   that pout like a
pink ladyslipper   those breasts brimming
in that thin blouse like two dollops of ice cream
in a glass bowl   those consonant knees
those assonant toes   that sassy butt
flash!   that pout opening: "Apples peaches
pumpkin pie   Screw a hundred boys before
I die!"

      You were a hive of rhymed couplets
      which I memorized—easily!

Those hot nights I couldn't sleep, I'd scoop
your glamour into myself as one scoops ice cream
into a bowl. I'd heap your libido into myself
as one heaps fresh fruits into a basket.

All fall, all winter, in dreary school,
I'd chant to myself: *Apples peaches pumpkin pie*
and my listening vulva would blossom
like an orchid.

> Oh, label me Lesbian if Lesbian means
> learning to love myself through first
> loving you.

snow   snow   snow
Snyder's Funeral Home a huge wedding cake
pink roses   blue larkspur   wearing white bonnets
all of us veiled by that blizzard
that Valentine's Day you married Death.

". . . kept fast company . . . caught a bad
disease. . . . What did I tell ya? . . .
died a dog's death."   Prick prick prick prick
my mother vaccinated me.

It didn't *take,* Maybelle.
I went right on swiping you.
With sheer concentration, I'd inhale you
through all my senses   puff out my pencil-
proportions with orbs of voluptuous pink
warm my ice-blue eyes to sapphires and drape
them with movie-star fringes.   Then, wandering
through the house, I'd meet in a mirror
that puny pastel girl.   *The mirror lied.*

I'd recoil into my chrysalis, where the moist
yearning would ferment once more:
Apples peaches pumpkin pie—
and I'd pump pump pump pump that skimmed-milk
girl into Creamy Fifteen.
It was easy.

Then tolling across my mother's face came
the worry my father slipped into a sigh:
"I declare! The image of Maybelle!"

> Beautiful bride, I caught your bouquet:
> Always in summer, I turn cold:
> Snow falls on all the flowers.

Willo's mother phoned juvenile court,
where a new clerk filed her complaint
under "Vandalism."   When Margaret's
mother was notified, she said,
"Shit! It's tit for tat!"

Their fumbling fathers shook hands.

Sweating boys prowled after them.
"Put a hotdog in her locker." "No, a big
carrot." "—two Coke bottles."
But when the boys met up with them in class,
all their acned faces just said "Hi."
The boys stopped short of peeking into
their windows, as planned, or following
them into the woods. What they were
afraid of finding was murder.

Slyly, silently, in corners all over
the school, on stairways, in parked cars,
other girls adhered in pairs. It was like
a courtship of snails.

"My daughter was raised in a Christian home!"
Willo's mother yipped. "That other girl's
a *witch!*"   Margaret's mother said "Shit"
and went on with her divorce.

Then Willo's mother would not leave the house:
"—ta think you would do this ta me
jest when I'm goin through my Change-o-Life!"
Her father ducked his worrybird face into
The Bible and came up with "Oh, Sisters!
We are living in The Last Days!"

But on the whole, this was a sensible place:
the Midwest; a sensible time: 1940. A lot of

people were trying hard to overcome their
narrow-mindedness. One by one, after school,
the teachers had talks with Margaret and Willo.
The psychologist gave them inkblot tests.
The blushing clergyman invited them to Youth Night.
The Girl Scout leader told them about Sublimation.
Listening with her lapful of Love, Willo wept.
But Margaret hauled her off with: "Why in Hell
sublimate the Sublime?"

That hurricane walloped all rescue efforts.
Then it lashed back upon itself, and stopped.
"Kill me!" Willo pleaded.   Margaret smuggled
her belladonna and razor blades and a pearl-
handled pistol: "Kill yourself, Lily Liver."
They remained knotted, plus and minus, in that
cold equation for a very long season.

Something *gave*. Margaret bounded out and
grabbed a wounded war veteran. He was
grateful for her guts.

Willo seemed stunned. Like a flower,
she waited for a kind man to transplant her.

He came: His smile was sunshine.
"What a poignant little face!"
His voice was rain.

He transplanted her.

She did not blossom.
His Kindness turned out to be sugar water.
It did not nourish her: it just preserved
the poignancy.

He dabbled in psychology books
and came up smiling with: "—But
you *couldn't* be: you're so *feminine.* . . ."
"—As far as I'm concerned, it never
happened."

She did not blame him.
She blamed herself: She had
married her fumbling father.

For many years,
her Rage was wrapped in Pity.

Then something wand-struck in her
flashed like a Loch Ness monster
through the sugar water.

He rushed her to a hospital
where this tale was born.

Apples

"Let me take you away from all this,"
he said.

> "From *this*?"
> She was a slight waif
> on scholarship from Appalachia,
> living on apples
> in an attic . . .
> writing poems.

He was a portly professor,
freshly bereaved, allotting himself
belated pleasures on his parents'
nest egg . . . like writing a novel.
"In Chapter One," he said,
"I introduce you as 'Sphinx,'
barefoot . . . too poor to own
even a dulcimer."

> "Lord."
> She smiled, seeming to listen
> less to him than to the
> seventeen-year cicadas.

By autumn
he yearned to rescue her from
anemia and shyness and superstitions.

> By winter,
> she wished at times to rest him
> from lugging his heavy hopes around.

> In spring,
> they married.

"Travel,"
he said, "is what you need."
Slung with cameras, tape recorders,
and transistor radios, surrounded with
lummox-luggage, sweating and smiling,
he looked like a big-game hunter.

>   In planes . . . in restaurants . . .
>   in theaters . . . in shops . . .
>   she sprouted phobias.
>   "I think I have radar," she whispered.

"Cocktails will help. Drink up."
All over Europe, all over Asia
he hauled her, passive as a papoose
. . . festooning her with Hindemith
and Picasso and Kabuki and Suzuki

>   until she was strangled in the
>   ticker tape of privileges.
>   *Travel?* she sighed,
>   and spelled it T R A V A I L.

"What you need is a good tranquilizer,"
he said.

>   When this laid her libido limp,

he said,
"A psychiatrist is what you need."

>   Thus, the therapy:
>   In London: "Professor, I'm afraid
>   you've caught yourself a pretty little
>   man-hater."

>   In Paris: ". . . an American neurosis."

27

In Tokyo: "Sir, are you asking me—ha!
to make a fat vessel for your fat needs
—out of this—ha! —*this divining rod?*"

In Washington: ". . . an awful lot of
early denial of oral needs."

In a Swiss chalet,
when she started to smile again,

he thought:
She needs a *baby*.

He gave her a whooping
cross-eyed daughter,
and while he was hustling
the madonna and child onto Kodachrome,
he added a thin, allergic son.

He grew thicker.

She, thinner.

The babies bawled.

"Have some steak.
Get it down with wine."

She nibbled apples.

The tots wailed.

He pumped out novels, lavishly.
One sold.
"No matter: Ahead of my Time."
He published privately.

Custodian to the clutter,
she wrote not one poem.

Years
they drifted
his statements . . . her silences
daft daughter . . . bewildered son
stuck one to the other by the thorns of his
optimism.

He grew so padded
and so florid of jowl
that his tie looked like
a tourniquet;

she, so wilted
that she looked crucified.

Brother and sister jangled.

"Lord."

He covered the moan
with the buzz of his typewriter.

Lord   Lord

It sounded to him
like the seventeen-year cicada,
returned.
He turned up the hi-fi.

Fat sister thwacked down
frail brother's paper airplane.
His fey gaze filled the house.

Lord   Lord

29

"What this family needs
is a smasheroo of a vacation."
He shuffled through sheaves
of brochures,

        Lord   *Lord*

phoned his broker,
phoned the airlines.

    The plane crashed on a mountainside.

        She woke   through mists
        remembering   "Too   poor   to   own
        even   a   dulcimer. . . ."

        Too rich.

        She walked away
        from generous death
        toward an apple tree
        and stood   barefoot
        on holy ground.

Afterglow

"I keep wondering what you do
with your anger," he said.

On the couch, she smiled.
"Anger? I have no anger."

He sighed.
She was a Garbo-woman, but small;
a *femme fatale*, one would guess at a glance,
yet she was a recluse,
orphan and exile, the daughter (she claimed)
of a raped nun who had died
giving birth in a prison camp.
He tried again:
"You've been coming to me
three times a week for nearly two years,
not like a patient with complaints,
but like a charming guest, a Scheherazade,
spellbinding me with your fantasies,
paying a high fee
yet asking nothing in return."

She shrugged.
She was wearing a violet sweater,
beige skirt, sandals.
Some days she wore a pale green sweater,
some days a blue one.
Never jewelry or cosmetics.
Just the clean pastel austerity.

"You've given so much," he said.
"I've given so little.
I fear such Sweetness."

"These have been the happiest hours
of my life. Your Listening has been
your Giving."

"I might believe that if the
burden of phobias you brought into
treatment had been removed—or even
diminished."

She smiled at the ceiling.
"You've eased me through a long
convalescence from Christianity . . .
and turned me toward Zen."

"Nonsense. You did that by yourself.
I'm no guru, nor do I wish to be one.
I'm just a man whose job is to help
release animal and infantile feelings.
I hate to think that when you leave
this room today, you'll retreat to
that garret to continue living like a
caged bird."

"The sky outside my window is full
of free birds."

He sighed again.
"I wonder, too, why you are choosing
this particular time to terminate therapy
—if, perhaps, a feeling toward me—
just a simple human feeling—is about
to come into the open?"
He was thinking of those women who
wept, or caressed the psychiatrist,
or stripped, or wrote him poems
(he was, they invariably moaned, too
handsome for this job) . . .

and of those other women who, after
a polite exit, started stalking . . .
or bled . . . or chose sleeping pills
. . . or slashed wrists.
"You still have ten minutes—in which
to tell me—or show me—how you *really*
feel."

She placed her hands on her cheeks.

"Don't be afraid. Just feel free to
do—what you want to do—"

Slowly, she sat up.

He leaned forward.

She stood.

He stood . . . opened his arms.

She looked surprised.

He smiled.

She turned away.
"Good-bye . . . and thank you."

The next week,
a new patient,
in the midst of his third session,
stopped talking, scowled, covered
his eyes and said,

"Gosh. I forgot what I was going to
say. All of a sudden, I got this far-
fetched fantasy. Why, it's silly!"

33

"Here, nothing is silly.
Or—if it seems silly—we use it.
What is this fantasy?"

> "Why—I see—or imagine I see—
> in your lap—this beautiful blond girl
> —in lavender sweater—light-colored
> skirt—sandals."

A month later,
another patient,
an older woman who had been coming
to him for years, faltered in her
usual chatter. . . .

> "That's odd. I keep seeing—flashing
> bright as lightning—this lovely blonde
> cuddling in your lap. She's wearing a
> lilac-colored sweater and— Why! She's the
> girl I used to see in your waiting room—
> the one I was so jealous of!"

The psychiatrist bought a new couch . . .
had the room repainted and recarpeted.

> "I keep having this dream," mused another
> patient, "about a beautiful blond girl
> in your lap—your daughter, it could be—
> dressed in a sort of orchid top and fawn
> skirt and—"

That was five years ago.
The psychiatrist has moved across the country.
Still, from time to time, a patient in his care
catches that same image.
Once it came as "a pale golden kitten
in a lavender sweater, purring in your lap."

34

Once, as "a baby girl in a violet sweater
and crocheted sandals."
—Uttered, in those cases, with a laugh of delight,
and clinging like a caul to the first
infantile fantasies. . . .
It comes most often, though,
to a patient later in therapy,
on the verge of erotic fantasies,
when it is tossed into their midst
like a bride's bouquet.

Kindergarten

Last born,
ectomorph,
having lived five springs
behind a honeysuckle-dripping wall
with sand
and crayons
and largo-purring tabby cat . . .
having slouched, day upon day,
for five winters,
with clogged nose and humid eyes
in the lap of his humming mother
in a larghetto rocking chair . . .
he stands in line now,
his cold hand in his mother's hand,
a clothespin-boy in a starched shirt,
gazing into the eyes of the other fives,
enduring the fortissimo.

*

Milk dribbled
from bent straws
is sour on plastic tabletops,
and his neighbor coughs cracker crumbs
onto his blue-veined cheek.
The circle, revolving around him
for "The Farmer in the Dell,"
is a whirling, swirling hell
of bubbling noses and chocolated molars
and breath
out of which he sends a drowning gaze
to Mrs. Bertram,
whose plump fingers plunk the piano
into a sound of storms . . .

whose large teeth (one gold)
shine savagely out of a big smile,
whose armpits, when she raises her hands
in exaggerated joy
at the end of the ordeal,
are two wet crescents . . .
   Oh, this social unit,
   this many-headed monster,
   spraying laughter, like gunshot,
   at his stomach, which he clasps
   with two soprano hands.

 *

Moving, ghostlike, at night
to the side of his parents' bed,
coughing artfully,
he receives the instant arms of his mother.
"Does a vet'narium have to know
how to play 'Musical Chairs'?" he quavers.
His father replies with a
swiftly turned rump
and a bearish grunt.
The mother rises,
spoons out cherry cough syrup,
and for the next hour
rocks her infant in the moonlit living room.
He whimpers quietly over school,
while she tries to argue, hypnotically,
in favor of games and groups.
It's like trying to entice the beads
of a glassed-in hand-puzzle
into shallow orbs.

 *

Other mothers
of squawlers and bawlers,
kickers and vomiters,

advise the firm hand
and the grinning departure.
But this mother,
who suffers the supermarket
as if it were a roller coaster,
and for whom P.T.A. is heavy traffic,
keeps a soft hand on this silent son,
whose tears trickle inward,
making polyped trachea
and clenched stomach
and pelleted stools.

*

The Christmas party:
Cookies crumbled in the clutched napkin . . .
the ever inner leak of tears . . .
the eye on the clock . . .
and the long afternoon at home
to lick the red lollipop
given to him, and only Him,
by a girl named Kitt.

*

Kitt:
Shimmering before the mother's eyes
like a new vitamin . . .
like a teddy bear
that might be borrowed
with hot chocolate
and fingerpaints and clay. . . .
The mother says,
"Shall we ask Kitt over some afternoon?"
"No!" he moans, chin aquiver,
"you know what she does now?
She yanks the earflaps down on my cap!"

*

Valentine's Day: Noon:
His mother, tight-lipped
outside the school door,
awaits the grieving face,
the napkin of untouched sweets. . . .
But no!
Here he comes, galloping,
wearing coat, lining-side out,
galoshes left behind,
waving a bag, like a banner,
and squealing,
"Look! Mrs. Bertram loves me . . .
and Pam . . . and Sam . . . and Susan
. . . and guess what? *Fourteen* of them
love me . . . and *Pam!*"

*

At the breakfast table,
where father and big sister
smack over thin bricks of ham
and twinned eggs,
the elf-boy
sips a doll-cup of Ovaltine
and toys with one graham cracker.
Beside him is a meticulously spangled
—blue—yellow—pink—violet—
Easter egg
for Pam.
The mother's pistol-presence
precludes teasing.

*

The school picnic finished,
he confers in his oak tree with Pam.

A limb above him,
in pink ruffled pants
and mosquito-bitten legs,
she calls down shrilly,
"Aren't you glad I chose you
to help pass out the cupcakes?"
He, gazing up at her frills—
oh, like a peony . . . a dahlia—
dangles from a branch below her.
"*Hey!* Aren't you *glad?*" she chirps.
Grinning over vacant lower teeth,
he pants, "Sure."

Apricot Light

An agnostic,
except in crises,
I held vigil one April evening
at the hospital bedside of my son.
"Viral pneumonia," the doctor had told us.
"No antibiotic for this type. We'll just
have to wait it out."

My ten-year-old Tad lay there,
making no more bulge in the white spread
than a note inserted into an envelope.
For a week, he had been coughing, coughing, coughing;
not eating;
for two days now, not even drinking.
Beside him, the tubed bottle dripped glucose
into his spindly arm;
behind him, the vaporizer hissed;
the twin equipment seeming to nourish not the boy
but that husk of harsh arfing
into which he had receded
like a forsaken puppy within a well of phlegm.

Paltry prayers wisped out of my head:
God, help my Tad—

Exhausted, I dozed
and saw   twitching on the wall
like a home movie
Christ in brown robe and sandals
surrounded by his disciples   who had
gathered up twelve baskets of leftovers
It was like an old Sunday School picture
animated
A balloon caption appeared above Christ's head

bearing some glyphs   which memory deciphered
"Go to your boat   and wait for me
I need to be alone"
The twelve   along with some stragglers
of the crowd   departed

Alone
Jesus started walking toward another hill
He moved slowly   pausing to lean on rocks
Clearly all that exponential multiplication
of the boy's five loaves and two fishes
had been strenuous
As he mounted the slope   he grasped the limb
of a tree   and a ballooned glyph appeared
"Tree   give me your energy"
He gripped a rock
"Stone   give me your strength"

An orangeness stained his fingertips
seeped into his fingers   his thumbs

Branch upon branch he grasped
bough upon bough
"Give me your strength"
A twig spurted a snake-tongue
"Yield me your secret"
A sapling glittered like a scepter

His fingers drank the orangeness   the goldenness
It flickered   amber-colored   in his palms

He climbed a little faster

Purple tinted the rocks
Indigo dyed the trees
Night laved the hillside

He came to a high boulder
wind-and-water-scooped into a shape
something like a lounge chair
Sinking into the crater   like a man
home from a hard day at the office
and placing his feet upon the ottoman-end
he sighed *"Mighty Rock   give me your power"*

He slumped   and slept
His slim thighs started soaking up the orangeness
His hips soaked up the coral-tinged yellowness
His buttocks drew it up
thick now   and rich   like honey
It glistened up the wick of spinal nerves
twinkled in his belly
fluttered through his ribs
flapped in his shoulder blades   like wings
winked in his ears   like earrings
danced in his skull
His face shone like a lamp

His elbows sipped
Bracelets of gold bubbled on the wrists
His heels drank
Bangles of amber on the ankles
necklaces of it   coral   topaz   peach
spilling from his shoulders
splashing into his lap

The rock-chair shimmered like a geode
throbbed like a throne

Below   above   all around   the indigo night
Center stage   all dazzling   all fulminating
a fountain   a geyser

The wall went blank. Intermission?

I glanced over at the bed
where my slight son was a bookmarker
in a closed book.
No arfing.
Just the dual gadgets murmuring.
My nipples ached with remembered colostrum.
God   God   plumed out of my breasts,
pull my poor puppy out of that well of phlegm—

The film resumed:

The Prince woke   yawned   stretched
His replenished flesh gleamed tawny-rose
as a ripe apricot
His auburn muzzle was gold-flecked from the feast

He stood   and stretched again
and looking up   he said Something to The Sky

A chandelier blossomed

I guess that was The Sky Answering

Christ laughed
Still a bit baubled with radiance
he started scampering down the hill
Chuckling   he juggled the lights
yo-yoed them into a hoop
swished it into a band
on which he cavorted like a tightrope walker

After a while   he stopped
shook his head   and frowned
He flapped some excess from his sleeves
wagged some from his frock
wrung tassels of it from his hem
stamped out the glow in the grass

When he resumed running
some sparkles still fringed him
like feathers on a looting fox

In his wake
the rocks were translucent   honeycombed
Clearly   Eons of Something had swarmed out of them
Boughs were bundles of hollow tubes
Fruits drooped like nursed teats
Leaves were lace   as if a billion larvae
had fed on them

At the foot of the hill
on the shore of the lake
a strong wind was blowing
The rascal simmered down to a walk

Now he was just a brown-robed figure
wafting across the blown tan sand

He paused   shielded his eyes
and studied the scene
The gale had huffed the little boat far
from shore   and was scooting it around
and around like a half-melon
the foam-fanged waves tasting it
the great greencurled tongues licking it

A dozen glyphed prayers

Then two dozen eyes looked out and saw
a ghostly something walking toward them
on the water   It was Christ

"—apricot juice—"

What? A sound track?

"Mom—"
through the hissing   through the dripping
"Mom—"
like the chirp of a cricket
waking in a winter crack

I turned
and saw in the shadow on the pillow
a something frail as a hepatica in a snowdrift
It was a smile
The wafer-hands swiveled on the wasted wrists
The praying mantis face turned toward me
"Mom, I want some apricot juice."

I found my feet
and wavered toward the ice bucket,
fumbled with a jug.
Juice gushed into the glass,
which I hitched to the feeble lips.
Tad sipped   and sipped.

Bells were gabbling
Above   below   all around
bells.
Sunrise was fracturing the window
yellow   orange   coral
into a flower.

Easter blazed into the room.

Low

1951

"I hafta count the cars," she says,
her hooked finger jabbing the November air.

    "Count the cars?" I say. "Why?"

"I hafta!" Her head pumps to assist the
finger: "—nine, ten, leven—"

    We stand shin-deep in snow,
    hunching under a renewed squall.
    Cousins, aunts, uncles, my sister Dora
    and her husband are straggling away from
    my dad's fresh grave.

    "But *why?*" I whisper
    as I take her elbow to steer her away.

She wrenches herself from me.
"Now I lost count!"
The finger finds the place in front of
her face and resumes the poking,
the head pumps more earnestly,
"—sixteen, seventeen, eighteen—Sikes n Agnes
always count the cars, and if I don't know how
many, they get mad."

    Sikes: her dwarfish oldest brother,
    pensioned after forty years of janitoring
    at the state asylum; hence an expert on
    the mind. Agnes, her oldest sister,
    yellowed and soured among doilies
    and Ouija board.

Embarrassed, I stand with her.
All the others have left.
The soggy flakes are chilling my shoulders,
but she is rooted here: the widow, age
fifty-nine, turned off, as ever, to her husband,
of whom she had said all those years his symptoms
were accumulating: *"His imagination; he'll outlive
me n marry a young woman with big tits. Agnes
says so."* —who babbled, even as he lingered,
a mere pelt stitched over his cancer, *"Brought
it on hisself. Brooded. Sikes knows a lotta
cases like that."*

The cars jerk away like starlings through the slushy
cemetery. I look down at the wet chrysanthemums
beside me.

   *"—twenty-four, twenty-five, twenty-
   six—Oh, I* hope *I got it* right.*"*

The toad-man stumps toward us: Sikes, made even
more top-heavy by hat and cigar: "Hey! Get in the
car, *you!"*

She flops along behind him like a hooked fish.
"Twenty-nine." She gulps. "No?
Maybe thirty?"

"You crazy?" he snarls. "Agnes got fifteen.
Why! You was countin the cars from that *other*
funeral!"

   Over my shoulder, I say good-bye to the
   wet chrysanthemums, then fold myself into
   the flivver with their bickering.

48

Agnes wags ochre jowls, fixes cinder-eyes
upon my mother. "Whassa matter with you, Katie?
It's fifteen."

Within that mound of urine-scented wine-
colored velveteen, I can feel that other
statement steaming (*"If you don't git holda
yerself, Katie, Sikes n me'll hafta put you
in the 'sylum"*). Before it can boil out of
her mouth, something fresh from the chrysanthemums
leaps from my tongue:

"Take her straight home," it says. "She needs
a rest."

They retreat like turtles—all three of them.

I should have known. No sooner am I alone
with my mother than she scolds,

"Won't ya never learn, you college girl? Ya
gotta make yerself *low*."

All evening, I watch her lips fumble through
that old pack of phrases for just the right
one to present to that pair when they drop in
to check on her tomorrow. I can guess what
it will be: *"I brought it on myself: You both
warned me more'n thirty years ago: that's what
I git fer marryin that GERMAN."*

1933
"Phooey!"
"That's what I think of it: Phooey!"
She snatches my all-A report card

from the kitchen table, whips it to her fanny,
and wipes.

Nellie, my schoolmate, cackles.
Her card is a bramble of D's.

With a spider-finger, my mother approaches
my long taffy-colored curls. She yanks one
loose, spits on it. "Buh! 'Beauty's only skin-deep!'"

Nellie, whose hair is the color of mud,
whoops her on.

> I hold my face rigid as a cameo.
> I am ten. For ten years I have been
> rehearsing for these scenes.

Later, after Nellie has left, my mother
will whisper, "I didn't spit hardly at all.
I don't want you gettin stuck-up. It's bad
ta git ahead o yer chums. Somethin bad always
happens ta them that use their mind too much.
In the biggest wing o the 'sylum, they're packed
in like cattle: doctors n perfessors that burned
out their minds." She taps her own tawny-brown
hair. "Runs in our family: Marks mostly them
with light hair."

> Fear? Anger? Shame?
> I feel a minimum.

Evenings, as I sit in the living room
across from my pale father and my dark sister,
he, silent with his Bible,
Dora, silent with her sewing,
I, silent with my schoolbook,
my mother will push a prodding finger

night, in bed, my husband scolded,
came for an abortion, not an exorcism."

hed. He was not watching through that lens.

My mother, in cahoots with those Skid Row
brothers, dreads those *other* males: boys
our age: Americans—tall, with white teeth
and cars. With her knee, she demonstrates,
repeatedly, just where to strike them, and *when*.
(She *knows*. Sikes showed her.)

My husband and our children had to endure
her only once, years ago, for twenty minutes.
They've spent as much time watching the
orangutan at the zoo. Cowed Dora
drags her brood to Grandma's every Sunday.

as from those twenty years of Sunday sessions
I yearned to yank the cord in Rena that might
ucker my own pouch of pain. "How about a farewell
ic on the Potomac?" I asked.

glacier-husband requested a tray in his den.
t and Tad exchanged that sneer.
Into the gouges scraped by those three exits,
ured sesame rolls, cheeses, Cold Duck,
ers, and songs.

a sunny rock by the Potomac,
the white mum in her hand, like a kitten,
ning . . . Rena loosened.
ough her voice, through her grimaces,
ing like pus through her gestures . . .
e the old woman, now eighty;
survivor of that family of ten.
w those mismatched eyes,

across the 'bituary page of the newspaper.
"Sara O'Conner. That could be the Sally O'Conner
that was my teacher. Seventy-eight; sure, that
could be her. Kidneys. All them O'Conners bloat
somethin awful with kidney trouble. . . .
She had it in fer me cuz my mother was dead
n my brother Dan put turpentine on her cat's
hind end. She called me 'Kitty' though she
knew my name was Katie, just ta cheapen me
fer the boys n she'd slap my hands with that
ruler cuz my eyes was funny n I talked
haff Dutch n I didn't wear nice dresses like
the Merican girls n Agnes n my brothers was
all so dark everone said there was nigger blood
in the family. Shit, Miss O'Conner, the meaner
ya got, the more I prayed fer ya. . . . *Clyde
Wagner.* Bet he's related to Henry Wagner.
That Henry stoned Sikes right on the head.
Sikes was bleedin somethin terrible, but he
just called out, 'Henry! Henry! I'm gonna pray
fer ya!'" She glares at my father, sticks
out her tongue. "It don't take no spirit jest
ta keep yer nose in the Bible. The real spirit
is when ya pray through yer own blood fer yer
enemy!" She thumbs her nose at my father.

He does not look up from the Bible.
Twenty years of rehearsals:
He's a better cameo than I am.

"Maude Moyer. My, my. Agnes worked in the
paper mill with a Maude Moyer, or Moynehan er
somethin like that. A real pretty girl: fair-
complected, nice teeth, big bust. Thought herself
above the mill gang, though . . . so she become
a Cathlic nun. Well, she started rammin them
candles up her you-know-what. She hit a certain

nerve that made her shake all over n that affected
the brain n she was put in the 'sylum. Sikes knows
all about those cases.''

We sit there, prim and pure
as three mirrors, tripling
the grotesqueries of this
turpentined Kitty.

1972

"This peacock-welcome for *that?*"
my husband whispered.

He was chagrined that I'd cut our prize
chrysanthemums for this round-shouldered,
twenty-year-old file clerk, picking her
acne, blinking at the carpet with that
familiar gaze. It was Dora's daughter, Rena,
who had smuggled herself a thousand miles,
by bus, for an abortion.

"She's a telescope to my own girlhood,"
I snapped, then choked back from him
that scene:

My mother's twin brother—rancid,
swarthy Klaus, leering at Dora's budding
sweater . . . lifting my skirt for a spank.
We flee to the kitchen; stand blinking at
the floor.   Mamma smirks. "I spose *you'd*
act better'n that if *you'd* been locked in
the Coop three years."
Dora and I exchange a sneer.
"Don't snub him," Mamma warns. "You may
have a son worse'n him someday." She dashes
to the pantry for boiled potatoes. "Run to

the cellar for a jar o wax be
We scurry.
"—An a jar o mustard pickle
jam!"
Last month: this feast for Ca
the game warden. Last summ
cottage cheese for Dan, near
canned heat.
"Don't tell yer old man!" Ma
At the stove a-sputter with sa
and potatoes and coffee and l
she starts rocking and stompi
her lullaby:
"Oh, the Niggers n the Irish
They don't amount to much—"
Klaus ambles to the kitchen ta
With spatula and spoon, she n
pat-a-cake motions to him.
"—But still they're better'n
the gol-darned Dutch!"
The paroled face splits like a r
fruit, showing brown stubs, lik
in mauve mush.
Her face splits, too, into tears.
He was her son long before we
her daughters.

Now I found myself whispering to my
and daughter, "Be kind to her, Tad . .
She hasn't had your privileges, Nart."

To thaw their frost, I brought out the
sparkling burgundy,
baked round loaves of bread . . . stuffe
picnic hamper . . .
sang old Dutch songs . . . coaxed Rena
sing, too.

saw those ochre jowls
stashed with that deeded venom,
saw those inverted lips nibbling,
heard her muttering:

"My Dora, she knows her place . . .
but you take that younger daughter—buh!
Got greedy fer college n that *high* stuff.
Married a perfessor: a Merican. He writes
poims.   *Suicide:* It's stamped all over
his face. . . .
Well, I brought it on myself: Hardly ever
punished her. When I did, her dad upheld
her.
With Dora, I did better.
It's easier ta hit a plain child.
But that second girl, she had me stumped.
She was so *fair* n dainty n she learned
so easy: just a baby when she could say
her numbers so clear . . . n the letters
n all the colors.
I admit it: *I was proud.*
Sikes saw it. Agnes saw it.
They warned me. They tole me ta whip
the piss outa her.
Just once would do it, they said.
Twice, at most, ta break that German pride.
But a mother's heart is soft.
Oh, I hit her a coupla times
when I caught her actin snippy
in fronta the lookin glass.
I hit her: just a *tap.*
Did she cry!
She'd have nothin to do with me after that.
Nothin.
Run to her dad fer everthing.
How's that fer bullheaded?

Two of a kind, them.
I was just dirt under their feet.
Never mind.
Oh, if I had it ta do all over again,
I'd whip—
No. You see sometimes in the paper
a poor mother that got started on her kid
n couldn't stop.
I tell you what: If I had it ta do
all over again n they was passin out them
bright little towheaded baby girls again,
I'd just say NO THANKS.
Course I pray for her. Night n day,
I pray fer that girl.
But the mistake's been made:
I was dumb. I let her put herself above me.
I s'pose she's still flyin high.
Of course, someone else will hafta do
what I dint do:
Sure. Someone will put her down *low*.
Just wait n see."
A slow shake of the head, a sigh.
"What I'm so fraid of is that it'll be
her kids that'll do it.
Yeah, it'll be her kids.
Just wait n see—"

Friday, with a yellow mum abloom like a sunrise
on her shoulder, Rena departed, by plane.

Saturday, our golden Nart,
playing the lead in the school play,
started to flounder on the stage . . .
slushed her lines . . . and flopped
like a hooked fish toward her brother
in the third row.

She sits now at the hospital window,
tapping her finger in front of her face,
pumping her head.
She's counting the cars in the parking lot.

Tad tells us, "I guess I gave her
some bad dope."

My husband has no comment.
Now he is the cameo.

I cannot sleep.
My bladder floods.
My crotch stings.

Mamma! Call off your prayers!

Wonders

Plants talk.
Else a spirit speaks through them.

One Sunday last month
in a greenhouse,
a glamorous plant all but beckoned to me.
I walked over to this pink flamboyance
that rose like a flamingo from a nest
of silver-brindled leaves,
and under my gaze, it flashed
into a crossbred *presence*—
pink cheeks, multiple blue eyes, tutu, feathers—
such as Picasso might skewer
and label "Ballerina."
This label, though, said "Aechmea fasciata, $25."
    —You Beauty, I thought,
    I wish I could have you.

    "IN THREE WEEKS," it whispered.
It was a voice, but not a voice . . .
more of a mist . . .
and something in me opened like a smile
to let it in.
    "IN THREE WEEKS," it insisted,
and light bloomed above me.
    —Wishful thinking, I warned myself.
Light and voice followed me out of the greenhouse
. . . "IN THREE WEEKS!"
encapsuled me like a bubble.

A few days later, Malcolm, my husband,
fell ill, and for many days I was too busy nursing
him to think of talking flowers.

The doorbell rang. It was his colleague,
holding in his arms—yes, the aechmea.
    Sunday. Three weeks, to the day.

Sitting here now with that Pink Beauty
and our secret, I confess this is not
the first flower that has spoken to me.
I remember when I was four, a big red zinnia
kept chanting . . . chanting? Well, *wafting*
a word: "JENNIE."
Then a woman appeared at our door.
Her face was round and rough and rosy,
like a zinnia.
"Come meet yer Aunt Jennie!" my mother called.
. . . Afterward, I announced,
"Mamma, the zinnia told me Aunt Jennie
was coming."
That Calvinistic finger wagged at me:
"I don't wanta hear that kinda talk."

Thus that part of me sank.

One hot, humid August afternoon,
when my husband and I were strolling along the canal,
a huge white mallow whispered to me from its
jelly-red center, "THE TREES ARE CLAPPING THEIR HANDS."
Stunned, I kept walking, and the red mouth called,
"THE TREES ARE CLAPPING THEIR HANDS! TELL MALCOLM."
I kept silent. I dared not risk it.
Minutes later, Malcolm halted: "Look!"
Beside the towpath, about three feet above the grass,
two small limbs were "clapping."
Still afraid to risk it, I said, "Maybe a spider
heard us coming—or some bees."

Malcolm replied, "No, it's not like that."
The two limbs went on clapping. Sumac, I think,
with leaves like fingers.
"Maybe a snake—" I offered.
Malcolm mused. "No, it's not that kind of movement."
He looked all around: "Not another leaf is stirring."
We stood watching the two little limbs.
It was not the random bouncing, the *bobbing,*
as from a retreating creature, but a *deliberate* action:
The two limbs were tilted out of their normal
horizontal position into the vertical,
and were patting together, regularly, like hands.
Exactly like hands.

As we watched, I was all but aware of
a smile above the limbs—
and a foamy white beard. . . .
I turned and lurched down the towpath,
that smile scorching between my shoulder blades.

Stones talk, too.

A schoolgirl, roaming one summer day
on Civil War grounds, I came upon a shambled
stone chimney.
"PLACE YOUR LEFT HAND ON ME," it entreated.
I did, and my fingers siphoned the message:
"I'M DANIEL THE DRUNKARD. PRAY FOR ME."
I all but saw a short man with scruffy red beard
and eyepatch. Nonplussed, I stumbled on
without praying.
>   —*Forgive me, Daniel.*
>   *I prayed when I got home.*

Street signs suffer.

Last year the big black letters
of the SANGMORE PLACE sign stared so mournfully
that I had to detour.
Two weeks later, in the newspaper,
the cause confronted me: *Young mother murdered.*
Baby cries to death in crib. Neighbors did not
want to interfere . . . Sangmore Place. . . .
My heart cracked. Grief gushed, and still
gushes for that baby.

Repeatedly, at Seminary Road,
the street sign seemed to sag with sorrow
. . . seemed to moan, "FOURTEEN!"
Week after week, when we passed it,
that sag, that ache, that moan: "FOURTEEN!"
A year later, on television, it came:
. . . *apartment building under construction*
at Seminary Road collapsed. . . . Fourteen
men trapped. . . .

SUTTON PLACE shuddered,
then signaled and signaled like a desperate
deaf-mute. A month later, news came that
our friend, Paul Sutton, had been killed
in a car crash.

Sangmore . . . Seminary . . . Sutton . . .
Why all these S's? I'm an S.
Are we all ticking together through
a kind of compassionate computer?
Have I already been shunted toward my exit?

Buildings speak, too,
or a spirit summons from them.

In May of 1964,
when I was trying to write a eulogy
for the May-born Jack Kennedy,
driving past The Department of Justice,
I saw—no, *felt*—someone waving to me
from that window to the left of the entrance.
Malcolm said, "What are you looking at?"
"The lovely trees," I lied.

A week later, the same thing happened:
that waving: so frantic, so urgent!
The impact must have jolted me, because
my small son asked, "What did you see, Mom?"
"The magnolia trees," I lied again.

Four years later, Robert Kennedy
was assassinated . . . and on television,
I saw The Department of Justice . . . saw the pointer
placed on the window—*the very window where that
SOMEONE had waved so urgently*—
heard the commentator say, "Office of The
Attorney General, Robert Kennedy—"

In May of 1972, when I was still struggling
with that eulogy, The Watergate, which I
passed occasionally, kept tugging at my attention.
Ship of Fools, I addressed it (which is what we
Democrats called that sumptuous building where
so many rich Republicans lived)—*what's with you?*
In my mind's eye, a face appeared,
big as a billboard, ruddy, white-whiskered,
gray-eyed.
Santa Claus? I mused, and the face
evolved into clarity: *Walt Whitman.*
". . . *I stop somewhere waiting for you* . . ."
and before I could fetch up the preceding lines

of his poem, a voice, like telepathy, intruded:
"DEAN . . . GEMSTONE."

In the ensuing weeks,
The Watergate wore Whitman's face
like a figurehead.
Names—"MITCHELL   CAULFIELD   COLSON"—
were beamed carefully, letter by letter,
as from a radio.
All summer, prophecies drifted—
"DEAN   NIXON RESIGN   L. KING WILL BE
PRESIDENT"—*
like vapor from something brewing.

So insistent the hum from that cauldron
that I wondered if The Watergate stands
on the spot where one hundred years ago
the May-born Whitman sat under his favorite
apple tree . . . looking out over the Tidal Basin
. . . dreaming of us Americans yet to be born.
. . . wondered, too, if, earlier, that Waver
at that window was Whitman, who had worked for
a while as clerk in the Office of The Attorney
General . . . wondered no more about The Clapper
at the canal. . . .
So sure my reception that I wondered
if the heat of my concentration on the
May-born Kennedy had melted the membrane
that let these messages through.

Flowers   trees   stones
        street signs   buildings . . .
And Whitman has returned, as he said he would.
"The Spirit bloweth where It will."

* Gerald Ford was born "Leslie King."

Often in mid-May, a week before my birthday,
It nudges me . . . breathes a malaise. . . .
It finds that sunken deadpan part of me;
then, like a yeast, It proliferates.
Through those soggy summer days and nights,
It pummels my wits . . . depresses me like mild flu
. . . swells and swells until It pushes up a cloth. . . .

I've never even hinted of it to Malcolm:
There's a coldness about him. . . .
And I don't want to bewitch my children.
But now that it's surfaced into fashion,
I'll slip these fragments to you, Stranger.

"Talk to your plants," say the current faddists.
I say, *Keep still. Listen.*

Sunshine

Golden God, where are You?

> Like a woman who watches from window
> to window for her lover, I wait for
> Your return
>   and watch
>   and wait.

You would not recognize me:

> Exiled on this northern island,
> I have dimmed to the celadon
> of Your least-loved Pisces.

> Depression has dragged my face
> into verticals.

> I'm wrinkled from Your withdrawal.

I did not realize I was addicted:

> My blondness depended on Your
> daily visit.

> For You, my eyes opened, like chicory.

> You kissed my nipples into glad pinks.

> My belly was buttoned to Yours
> in noons of joy.

> I was Your easy lay.

Here we huddle in a cave of clouds.

My husband sips glow from wines.
Teas and coffees comfort him.

I am not adaptable.
Alcohol dallies me.
Caffeine increases my sea-hag scowl.

I must shake this fidelity; I must rebound.

I've gazed long at Rainier,
but he is remote, his moon-shoulder
shawled in snow.

I took my Sulk for a walk;
The Surf flopped its sops at my feet.

I turned my Sneer to driftwood-dragons
and found a good groin, which I
stroked   straddled

but it was too freaky to play.

Hooked, I twist on the spit of remembered
Radiance,

       and twist
           and twist.

Lover? Did I sometimes shield myself
from You?
—salve myself against Your intensity?

Where are You now?
      Are You caressing Colorado?
        mounting Maryland?
          flooding Florida?

Sunny?

How about
some
cold turkey?

Whelping

"At last!"

Your baritone nicks me . . . then
your familiar grin.

Your hand gallops toward mine.

I recoil.

He thinks when he pressed her doorbell
she walked twenty steps from her study?
Wrong. A thousand miles Up/Down, she
crawled out of a den, shook off quills,
ripped out fangs . . . and as she stumbled,
slapped this smile under her snout,
clapped in this tongue . . . to pronounce:

"Hello?"

"I've traveled *eons* to reach this
island of yours!"

—had first unnippled a fuzzy simile,
unlapped a mewing metaphor.

You squint to slow down the reeling of
my wintered face into your mind.
"I traced you through your poems—
in magazines."

Trapped . . . I lead you toward this
upholstery. Your aura snags mine.

". . . Have you been ill?"

Your voice scrapes my jugular. You
don't know that Mr. Muse loves the
wounded woman:

He stalks along the Edge,
watching for that One most sloshed
by the status quo. Gently He'll lick
her wry smile, and if it bites back,
He'll bash her wound into a womb.

". . . You've been ill."

My glance has sagged through your
monologue. "Mmm?" You expected the
schoolgirl-me, her attention a tram-
poline for your patter. My lip curls:
"Ill?" Is that croak mine? "You
could call it *ill*."—But a Heaviness
settled. The net split—

She tucked the tatters, somehow,
into a kind of pouch. Where her
attention had been concave, it turned
convex. *"Dazed!"* her husband groaned,
and consigned himself to groceries and
neighbors.

"You seem—depressed."
Your squint is a stethoscope.

"Mmm? Well, tired—"

Unsnapped from the mundane, she
crouched in that pouch . . . which
soared like a balloon into Strangeness
. . . and slipped. It was on that Brink
Mr. Muse found her.

You drag the stunned-me around in
your skull. "—A sort of drop-out,
I'll bet—"

           I bare my teeth. "Last year, in-laws
           dropped in—" (The fat prose is rotting
           in my net.)

"I'm groping for the word—"
Your gaze pries my fist. "'Recluse?'
'cloistered?'"

           "They took us to a wedding." (I'm still
           mopping up the oil slick.)

Your glance strays kitchenward—

           to be trounced by mine. "'*Farouche.*'
           Is that the word?"

Eyes downcast, you taste the term,
and nod. "Would you—could we—
maybe walk on the beach?"

           Let her lean toward him with the
           lightest breath of *maybe,* and Oldman
           Muse will flip her gullet upside down
           to fart:

           "No thanks." *My poor whelps!*
           Flubbing their finny wings—

You rise, and your feet falter toward
the door. "I tried—I mean— You're
not in the phone book."

           "Unlisted," I snarl. "And I don't
           answer it." I'm twitching to flush

you from my cochlea . . . to snort you
out of my nares—

"I should have written you—"

"In fact, my answering the doorbell
was an accident: I thought it was my
husband, who'd lost his key."

Your hand grabs out of your drowning
and locates the doorknob.

My darlings! Here I come!

Whitey

"...just a line to let you know
Mom had a heart attack yesterday.
Hate to scare you but at her age . . . Dora."

The words lurch on the page.

I've been expecting this message.
That's the real reason I don't answer the phone.
My mother is eighty-five.
She is three thousand miles from here.

I grasp these posts to regain my balance.

But I cannot eat. I cannot sleep.

It's a sweltering summer day.
We're riding in a streetcar:
my mother, Dora, and I.
My mother is scrawny and sallow,
with frizzy taupe hair,
those freaky eyes focused in her lap.
Dora, who is ten, is swarthy,
with crimpy black hair and brown eyes.
I am five, thin, towheaded, gray-eyed.

My sister and I are picking our noses.
Mamma whacks Dora.
Strangers twist in their seats to glower.

Mamma crouches toward the women across
the aisle: "I don't hit Whitey.
She hasn't got long ta live."

Home, in our little brown bungalow, I droop.
"Don't brood," Mamma scolds.

Those eyes—one brown, one gray—watch me.
"I jest *said* that. I was havin a spell
with my nerves n sumpin come over me
n I *said* that."

Days later, I'm still drooping.
"I *told* ya!" The witch-stare warns me.
"I jest made it *up!*"

Dora found a chum to cuff her around.
I languished on the couch.

In kindergarten, with hands folded, lips locked,
I was no more trouble than a trillium.
The teacher coaxed me into motion with crayons,
nourished me with praise.

Then another summer clamped down, like a lid,
and again, I receded to the couch.

I think that was the summer Mamma
jabbed a paring knife into Dora's shoulder:
"Fer teasin Whitey! *That's* why!"

"Pray for one another," sighed our ashen father,
and departed, dinner pail under his arm,
for the railroad.

"Eat!" Mamma begged me. "I don't know what'll
b'come o ya if ya don't *eat!*"

I turned my face to the wallpaper.

"Hey!" she huffed, "how's bout some chin-pie?"
She knelt beside me and started stroking her

sharp chin across my cheek. "Tell me what ya hate!"
she wheedled. "Come on! *Tell* me."
        that sourkraut-breath sneaking across my nostrils,
        that cudgel-chin digging at my jaw—
"Nope? Then I'll tell *you* what *I* hate:
It's them high muckety-mucks."
        grinding at my collarbone
"You know: a person that thinks their *strundt*
don't stink. Aw, come on, Whitey. It's *yer* turn.
What d'ya hate, huh? *Huh?*"
        the chin prodding and prodding my pallor
I dreamed up a smooth mother.
I pictured her moving into the stucco house
across the street: a stylish lady
with calm light hair and matched doll-eyes.
"Dora! Wilhelmina!" she'd call in a creamy voice.
She'd be standing on her porch, smiling,
smelling like the art teacher.
She'd ask us to take care of her cats while
she went away with her husband, or someone.
"—and help yourselves to lunch!"

"Eat! Whitey! *Eat! Eat! EAT!"* Mamma chanted.
"Ya want the wind ta blow ya *away?"*
And her flatulence dittoed her distress.

By the Fourth of July—I dreamed . . .
Surely before Labor Day . . . she'd appear:
this surrogate mother for whom lunch was no crisis,
whose bowels were not fastened to my behavior.

But summer after summer, it was the same:
In August, when she had scratched away the small
gloss of school, Mamma would struggle up out of

her affliction like a wounded beast out of its lair
and make us board that streetcar with her "ta buy
youse a school outfit."

Cowering through the shops,
that grotesque glance nabbing the crowd,
she'd sputter, "Stuck-up Mericans!"
   her armpits reeking panic
"Ridin fer a fall!"

Steered by her clammy claw, I'd paddle through
nausea dense as pond scum.

   Through a greenish membrane, I audienced
   my classmates: When Barbara's mother picked her
   up after school for dancing lessons, she fondled
   Barbara's curls: "Honey! You look so pretty!"
   After the Christmas program, Shirley's mother
   hugged her: "Sweetheart! You sang like an angel!"

One summer Mamma drove a hatpin into her wrist.

"Oh, Sisters!" my father sniveled, tucking his Bible
into his dinner pail, "this is what we have to expect
in The Last Days!" And the screen door blammed behind him.

Enter khaki-colored, pillow-lipped Uncle Klaus,
on parole from prison, followed by vinegar-colored,
bushy-haired Casey, laid off from the mill.

"It's *Whitey!*" Mamma bleated.
"I'm worried ta *death* over *Whitey*."

Hunched at the kitchen table, the pair proceeded
to dose Dora and me with the saga of the family-
sufferings:
"Nobody'd bleeve ye vuz from da Nedderlunds."
"'Nigger in da voodpile!' dem Yankees vould holler."
"N 'Touch a da tarbrush!'"
"'Hey, Coon!' dey'd holler. 'Hey, Crow!'"
"'Crazy-Eyes' dey called yer mudder."
"Tink dat don't jar yer slats?"

Two uncles, mother, sister, all downcast,
all dusky, like Van Gogh's potato eaters—
no, *duskier*—they crouched around me—pristinely blond
like my father's mother . . . turned four gazes, like
beggars' cups, upon *me*, The Lily, youngest of the clan,
as if the smudge had at last burnt itself out in ME.

"Vhitey'll mount ta sumpin," Casey proclaimed.

Mamma thumbed her nose. "When it comes ta *backbone,*
Whitey can't hold a candle ta Pickanniny."

In school, I started confronting a compliment
as if it were a curse. Let a classmate exclaim,
"I'd give anything for your *brains*, Wilhelmina!"
I'd pull a wry mouth: "I'd give anything for *your
health!*" Let someone sigh, "What lovely platinum
hair!" I'd whirl like a ballerina: "Look! It's
dark in back!"

Pivoting on praise, flaunting flaws:
I had touched magic. I was turning into
a kind of peripheral princess.

But always that awful spiral of seasons pitching me down
from my domain, plunging me into those cauldron-summers
with Mamma.

My all-A report card was a diamond I had to swallow
on the way home. Upon entering the bungalow, I'd
collapse, pale and dizzy, onto that couch.

My ailment accused her. Her worry wrung me.
We marinated in that mutual misery.

I'd lie there making the wallpaper bloom
that Renoirish neighbor. *Now*, I'd pray.
If she comes now, it's still not too late.
Now. Let her come: This woman who likes
her life. NOW while I'm still unstained—

But the summers came and went, came and went,
pinch   pinch   pinch

Then came the summer that trapped me.
I was twelve.
My backbone seemed stitched to that couch.

The doctor pricked a TB test into my forearm.

Coffined on that couch, I sank down down down
through mauve mists   down down through darkness
down into muck   and stayed   and stayed.

The three dots failed to swell like peas.
The doctor shrugged: "She'll be better
when school starts."

In a kind of fever   a kind of delirium   in an
awful heat   I started sprouting   started climbing
up   up   like a clematis   up up up   a snow-white
clematis   I saw myself leaving here someday
for college   for marriage   and on a distant day
returning   transfigured   Adult   Angel
with Radiance to heal ALL

I guess it was then my wraith-body started pumping
out those poems.

A scholarship swept me away.
"—*lacking Pride, they went for Pity, like a pack of
hyenas for leftovers*—" was a line of a freshman poem.
Swoosh! A second scholarship.
"—*I dreaded catching my mother's madness, like flu*—"
went a sophomore poem.
A sequence of scholarships swooshed me away some more.

Then a princely young foreign correspondent swooped
me away *for good*.

Dora's letter nudges me:
"—hate to scare you but at her age—"

It's November 1951. My squeamishness subdued
with tranquilizers, I've descended for a day into
that sooty hometown for my father's funeral. . . .
Ducking her head deferentially as I make my hasty
exit, Mamma addresses my black Parisian veil:
"Sometimes I'd like ta see yer house, Whitey—"
thrusting up her palm like a STOP sign—

"Not *company*. NO! But like a *mouse*, just ta
peek at yer dishes n things n yer rugs—"

Oh, Mamma.
Always—in London, in Paris, in Tokyo,
in Oslo, in Amsterdam—I've paddled through
pond scum.   For my children, often that
greenish membrane.

"Dear Dora," I write

> *In poems   all these years   and only*
> *in poems   have I   occasionally*
> *digested   the   chin-pie.*

Dear Dora—

> *Do I pack the black veil   and swallow*
> *the sequence of pills   and descend*
> *once more   the zombie?*

Dear Dora—

> *This salutation   stains this stationery*
> *like mouse turds.*

Dear Dora—

> *Or do I   fly back to you   Mamma*
> *bearing   your Madness   like a torch?*